Q READS

DIMES TO DOLLARS

TERI THOMAS

SADDLEBACK
EDUCATIONAL PUBLISHING

QREADS

SADDLEBACK
EDUCATIONAL PUBLISHING
www.sdlback.com

ISBN-13: 978-1-61651-217-0
ISBN-10: 1-61651-217-2
eBook: 978-1-60291-939-6

Printed in the U.S.A.

21 20 19 18 17   3 4 5 6 7

■ ■ ■

Anna Torres and Toni Boucher sat in the observation deck of the *California Zephyr*. The clickity-clack of the train's wheels was music to their ears. At last they were on the first leg of their long-awaited camping trip.

The two 20-year-olds were best friends. After high school, they'd trained to become CNAs, or certified nursing assistants. Then they'd gotten jobs at the same convalescent hospital. Helping people fight their way back from serious injury or illness was rewarding work.

The fun-loving girls were popular with both the staff and the patients—especially the elderly. Because Toni and Anna were always willing to listen, many old people had shared their fascinating stories with them.

■ ■ ■

Anna and Toni had been planning this trip for more than a year. Toni couldn't wait to climb mountains and camp out under the stars. Since Anna was crazy about animals, she wanted to see plenty of wildlife. After hours of discussion, they'd chosen Colorado as the perfect destination.

Their adventure had finally begun the day before. After departing from Sacramento, California, their hometown, the train had slowly climbed the Sierra Nevada Mountains. Then it sped across the high-desert plains of the Great Nevada Basin. Despite their excitement, the girls had fallen asleep around 11:00 P.M., shortly after passing through Elko, Nevada. They were jolted awake early the next morning as the train pulled out of Provo, Utah. After having a leisurely breakfast in the dining car, they took seats in the observation deck. The huge, panoramic windows there offered spectacular views of the Rocky Mountains.

■ ■ ■

Toni dug into her backpack and pulled out the train schedule. "We crossed the state line about an hour ago," she said. "We should be getting to Silver Springs in a couple more hours. Then let the adventure begin!"

"Look, Toni! There's a bald eagle!" Anna cried out excitedly. "And there's another one!"

Toni gazed at the sight in wonder. "I see them," she said.

Anna brushed her long, dark hair aside to adjust her binoculars. Now the train was passing through a narrow canyon. "There must be an aerie around here someplace," she said as she leaned forward to get a closer look.

Toni's intense green eyes flickered with interest. "An aerie? I've never heard that word before. What's that?" she asked.

"It's an eagle's nest," Anna explained. "Bald eagles use sticks and branches to build their aeries at the tops of tall trees or in the cracks of cliffs. That way, predators can't get to the eggs. The eagles come back to the same spot year after year, making their aerie bigger each time. Old aeries are sometimes 20 feet wide and can weigh as much as 4,000 pounds!"

"You sure do know your animals, don't you?" Toni said with admiration.

Anna was pleased with Toni's compliment. "And you also have an eagle eye for spotting eagles!" Toni added with a giggle.

Anna laughed at her friend's silly play on words. "I really do find eagles fascinating," she said. "Did you know they mate for life, and that the male and female take turns watching the nest? I love to watch them swoop through the air, so alive and free."

"Oh, yeah. Those two surely were a spectacular sight," Toni agreed.

"There aren't all that many bald eagles left in the lower 48 states," Anna continued. "That's why it's so exciting to see a pair so soon after we arrived in Colorado."

"It's sad that they've become so rare," Toni sighed. "Wouldn't it be awful if the proud symbol of our country became extinct?"

Anna nodded. "It sure would," she said. "But bald eagles have been making a strong comeback lately. In fact, they were just recently taken off the threatened species list for the lower 48 states. There are still lots of eagles up in Alaska and Canada, though. Most of the bald eagles living in the wild today can be found up there."

■ ■ ■

Toni dug in her backpack for maps. "Come on, Anna," she said. "It's time to do some planning."

The girls spread the maps out as best they could and started chattering.

Suddenly, a voice interrupted them. "You girls on a vacation trip, or are you here looking for treasure?"

Anna and Toni looked up. An old man with a long, reddish-white beard was sitting across the aisle from them. "We're on vacation," Toni said brightly. "We're going to camp out near Silver Springs for a few days and do some mountain climbing. I'm Toni Boucher, by the way, and this is my friend Anna Torres."

"Smithson Jeffers here," the old man said with a friendly, toothless grin. "But you can call me Smitty like everyone else does. Sounds like you've got a mighty fine plan."

Toni was curious. "What did you mean about treasure hunting?" she asked.

Smitty smiled. "There's an awful lot of interesting history around these parts," he explained. "Did you know the famous outlaw, Doc Holliday, is buried in Glenwood Springs? That's just up the road a bit from Silver Springs. Heck, this was the wild, wild West only about a hundred years ago! Back then a lot of newcomers were trying to strike it rich in the mines. It was a pretty rough place back in those days."

Anna smiled. "You sound like you remember it personally," she teased.

"Well, now, I'm not quite *that* old!" Smitty laughed good-naturedly. "I just happen to like the old stories. And this area has produced some great ones!"

"And some of that history has to do with treasure?" Toni prodded.

"You bet it does!" Smitty grinned. "Have either of you two girls ever heard about the famous stagecoach robbery that happened here? That story goes back more than a hundred years."

Both girls shook their heads.

"Well, then, let me tell you all about it," Smitty chuckled.

■ ■ ■

Smitty settled back in his seat and began his story.

"Seems a stagecoach loaded with silver dimes was robbed back in March of 1898. The stagecoach was going through Silver Springs Canyon—right where we're heading now. The shiny new dimes were fresh from the Denver Mint. That's where new coins are made, you know.

"Anyway, all those dimes were supposed to be delivered to Salt Lake City—but they never made it. A bandit by the name of Cole

Drake and four of his henchmen saw to that. They robbed the stagecoach at gunpoint. Then they took a load of dimes and headed up the canyon on horseback.

"It wasn't long before the sheriff was hot on their trail," Smitty went on. "The posse caught up with them at the end of the canyon. But Drake and his men didn't give up without a fight. After a fierce shootout, all the bandits were dead. But the dimes were nowhere to be found. The sheriff figured the bad guys must have stashed them somewhere along the way."

"So you're saying that the dimes were never recovered?" Toni asked.

"That's right—they never were," the oldtimer said. "Not that a whole lot of folks haven't given it a try over the years. I've even hunted for the dimes myself a time or two. But that posse covered a lot of ground. They chased those darn robbers the full length of the canyon! Drake and his men could have squirreled away those dimes almost anywhere."

"That's a great story," Anna said. "But how could some sacks of dimes add up to a *real* treasure?"

"Well," Smitty replied, "there were a whole lot of dimes—about $35,000 worth, as a matter of fact."

"About thirty-five thousand dollars, huh?" Anna pondered. "With inflation, those dimes would be worth well over half a million dollars today. Probably closer to a million, I'd bet."

"That's right," Smitty agreed. "And dimes were nearly pure silver in those days. The U.S. government stopped minting silver dimes in the 1960s. Nowadays they're made from nickel and copper instead. So silver dimes are valuable to coin collectors. And these dimes would be even *more* valuable because of their history. After all, they're booty from a famous robbery!"

"Hmmm," Anna mused. "Maybe we could look around for the dimes while we're camping in the canyon."

"Good idea, Anna. Let's do it!" Toni said

enthusiastically. "Oh, boy, we're going on a treasure hunt!"

Smitty laughed. "As I said, a lot of other people have searched for the dimes without finding a darned thing. But who knows? Maybe you'll have beginner's luck!"

"You're right, Smitty," Anna said. "We probably *won't* find the dimes—but it couldn't hurt to try! Besides, it would just add more excitement to our adventure."

"Dead Man's Point might be a good place to start," Smitty suggested. "It's off the beaten track."

"Why would a place be called Dead Man's Point?" Toni asked curiously.

"There was a lynching there back in 1885," Smitty said sadly. "A mob of ranchers hanged a suspected cattle rustler. Turned out the fellow didn't even do it. The sheriff caught the real rustler red-handed. But it was too late for the poor drifter who got blamed."

"That's really awful," Anna said. "This area must have been pretty lawless back then, huh?"

"Yup, it sure was," Smitty agreed. "Well, I hope you ladies have fun on your adventure. It was a pleasure meeting you both!"

"You, too, Smitty!" the girls chimed in. "Good luck to you, too!"

■ ■ ■

Anna and Toni stood on the platform of the train station in Silver Springs. Their gear was piled up beside them. "Well, which will it be?" Toni said as she hoisted her heavy pack onto her back. "Lunch, or do we head straight into the canyon?"

"Lunch—*definitely*!" Anna replied. "I'm starving."

The two girls gathered up the rest of their gear and headed toward the main street of town.

"Look at that old hotel," Anna said. "It's got a patio cafe where we can eat outside. That'll make it easier to deal with all of this bulky gear."

The girls found an empty table near the street. They leaned their packs against a thick adobe wall that surrounded the small cafe.

Toni looked around. The cafe was decorated with rusty old mining tools and cracked leather saddles. There were even some old boots with plants growing out of them. "This place is great!" Toni said. "Look at all the neat stuff they've got around here. There's even an old covered wagon over in that corner. Maybe we can use it to haul the dimes after we find them."

"I thought you were eager to start mountain climbing!" Anna said with a laugh. "But Smitty's story about that old stagecoach robbery really *was* fascinating! I can't wait to start looking for those dimes either. And even if we don't find them, a treasure hunt will still be a good way to kick off our camping trip."

"Afternoon, girls," a deep voice said.

Toni and Anna looked up to see two good-looking guys about their age. Standing on the other side of the low adobe wall, they were dressed in faded jeans and cowboy boots.

The lanky, sandy-haired cowboy leaned over the wall and smiled. "I'm Pete Walker," he said, "and this is Steve Connors. We're ranch hands out at the J-Bar-K cattle ranch. We couldn't help overhearing your conversation. Mind if we join you?"

Toni and Anna looked at each other. A silent question passed between them. Then Anna gave a small nod.

Toni turned back to the two young men. "Sure," she said. "We're about to have lunch."

Pete and Steve came into the patio and grabbed a couple of chairs from another table. After the server took their lunch order, Anna broke the ice.

"Are you guys from around here?" she asked.

"Born and raised," Pete smiled. He had warm brown eyes and rough, calloused hands. "We were interested in what you gals were saying about the stagecoach robbery."

"Yes, we heard about it from a man named Smitty we met on the train," Anna replied. "We just got off the train from California."

"California, huh?" Steve smirked. "We get a lot of tourists from there—yuppies who come out here for the *ambience*," he continued sarcastically.

Toni and Anna looked at each other. "Actually, we came here to go camping and mountain climbing—and also to check out the wildlife," Toni said defensively. "But after hearing about the stagecoach robbery, we decided a little treasure hunting might be fun."

"Yeah, everybody around here has heard that story a thousand times," Steve snickered. "And lots of people have looked for those dimes, too. You girls might as well forget about your silly treasure hunt. If you ask me, it's a waste of time."

Both girls were annoyed. "Well," Anna said gruffly, "we *didn't* ask you, did we?"

Pete glared at Steve and then turned back to the girls. "Please let me apologize," he said. "Steve seems to have left his manners back at the ranch." He gave the other man a kick under the table.

Just then the server put down their plates. For a few minutes, they all enjoyed their hamburgers in silence.

Anna finished hers first. "Anyway, we're certainly not getting our hopes up about finding the money," she said. "We just thought it wouldn't hurt to look."

"Sure, nothing wrong with a little added excitement," Pete said. "Where are you planning to start looking?"

"We thought we'd hike over to Dead Man's Point," Toni said. "Smitty said that would be a good place to start."

"He's right," Pete smiled. "Dead Man's Point isn't all that far from where the stagecoach was ambushed. I've actually done quite a bit of research on that robbery. As a hobby, my family's spent a fair amount of time looking for those dimes. We've been through Dead Man's Point lots of times. But we never found a single dime. Still—you never know."

"I've been thinking about the robbers being on horseback," Anna said. "They wouldn't have been able to go up a sheer cliff or down a really steep ravine. So maybe we'll stick to the canyon floor."

"That's a good point," Pete said. "I remember reading that the dimes weighed nearly 2,000 pounds! Drake and his men had a few extra pack horses. But still, the weight of all those dimes must have really loaded down those poor animals. Drake must have known they'd be too slow to outrun a posse. So, I'd bet they hid the dimes not too long after the robbery. Once the dimes were stowed, they could lead the posse on a wild goose chase. Then, after they'd lost them, they could go back for the loot."

Anna was impressed. "That sure sounds reasonable to me. You've really done your homework, Pete!" she said.

"Like I said, my family and I have had some experience looking for those dimes," Pete said bashfully.

"Hurry up, Pete," Steve interrupted rudely. "It's time to hit the road."

Pete looked at Steve and sighed. *The next time I meet some pretty girls,* he thought to himself, *I'm going to ditch Steve fast.*

He turned back to Anna and Toni. "Would you like a ride—at least part of the way?" Pete asked. "My truck's parked just across the street, and we were headed in that direction anyway." He pointed to a very battered old turquoise-colored pickup.

"No, thanks—we came here to do some hiking," Anna said. "But maybe we'll see you guys around."

After they left, Toni heaved a sigh of relief. "That Steve was a first-class jerk," she grumbled.

"I couldn't agree more! But Pete seemed like a real sweetheart," Anna smiled. "I wouldn't mind at all if we ran into him again."

■ ■ ■

The next morning a blood-red sun rose over Silver Springs Canyon. The afternoon before, Toni and Anna had hiked several miles into the gorge. They'd finished setting up camp just as the sun started to dip behind the dark and shadowy canyon walls.

Over the next few days, the girls hiked farther and farther as they worked their way toward Dead Man's Point. They kept an eye out for the dimes, but both of them knew it was like looking for a needle in a haystack. They didn't let the search interfere with their real reason for being there.

The trip had been wonderful so far—everything they had imagined. They'd made some really exciting climbs. And while at first glance the land seemed barren and desolate, they had seen a variety of wildlife. Anna was thrilled.

"Hmmm," Anna said, peering through her binoculars. "It looks like that might be an aerie up ahead—on the ledge of the canyon wall. From here it looks like we could get to it without too much difficulty. Let's go check it out!"

"Wouldn't it be dangerous to go too near an aerie?" Toni asked nervously. "Being attacked by a bald eagle isn't high on my list of fun-filled activities."

Anna laughed. "Well, I don't think that

aerie is being used right now," she said reassuringly. "If eaglets were there—or even just eggs—either the mother or father would be with them. Both parents wouldn't leave the nest at the same time. Don't worry, Toni. I think we're pretty safe."

As the girls neared the nest, Anna pulled out her binoculars again.

"Yep, it's definitely an aerie," she said excitedly. "I don't see any eaglets or parent eagles around. Bald eagles usually lay their eggs in March. If this one were being used, there'd be eaglets in it by now. I think this nest must have been abandoned."

"Okay. I guess it'd be safe to climb up for a better look, then," Toni agreed.

The girls shouldered their climbing equipment and started to work their way up the wall of the steep cliff.

■ ■ ■

"This aerie must be at least 15 feet wide!" Anna exclaimed. "And judging from all the moss on the sticks, I'd say it hasn't been used for years."

Toni climbed into the center of the nest. Flapping her arms, she cried out, "*Squawk, squawk.* Feed me!"

Anna laughed at her friend's silly antics. "Get out of there before you hurt yourself," she warned her friend.

But Toni was having too much fun. She crawled toward the edge of the nest shouting, "Time to fly. Catch you later. I'm out of here." From her lofty perch, she looked down toward the canyon floor.

"Oh, look!" she cried out.

"What?" Anna said. "Are you okay?"

"Yeah, I'm fine," Toni replied. "But you've *got* to see this!"

Anna crawled across the nest and joined her friend. They both peered down at the entrance to a cave. It was almost hidden behind a cluster of huge rocks.

"Wow! A secret cave!" Anna said. "From anywhere but up here, you'd never know that cave was there."

Anna reached for her binoculars and took

a closer look. She could just make out an old cloth bag stamped with the words U.S. MINT.

"Omigosh!" Anna screamed. *It's the dimes!*"

Just then Anna spied a turquoise pickup at the bottom of the cliff. It was Pete and Steve! Both girls waved their arms and shouted, "Up here!"

"They see us!" Toni said. "Come on. I can't wait to tell them."

■ ■ ■

"**I** thought we might find you ladies up here!" Pete greeted them with a beaming smile. "Since it's Saturday, we thought you two might like to go with us to a dance—"

Before Pete could finish, Anna threw her arms around him and gave him a big hug. He grinned at the unexpectedly warm greeting. "Oh, Pete, I'm so glad to see you!" she exclaimed. "You won't believe this. *We actually found the dimes!*"

"Yeah, just this very minute!" Toni added excitedly. "There's a cave behind that cluster of rocks over there. We spotted it from the eagle's nest."

Pete's mouth dropped open. "Holy cow!" he exclaimed. "Let's go look!"

The four of them searched around the cluster of rocks for a few minutes. Then suddenly, Pete shouted, "Hey, over here!" The others ran to him.

"Boy, if you didn't *know* this was here, you'd never find it," Steve said.

A few moments later, they all stopped in their tracks and stared. *A big pile of burlap sacks lay just inside the mouth of the cave.*

■ ■ ■

Toni whistled in amazement. "Just look at all those bags!" she whispered. "Altogether, there must be 40 or 50 of them."

"Yeah," Pete said, "40 or 50 bags in very poor condition. We'll have to go back to town and get some sturdy crates to move them."

"Yes," Anna said, "and notify the sheriff. I imagine he'll want to contact the Treasury Department."

"No, I don't think we'll do that," Steve said. His voice was oddly flat—and threatening.

Pete and the girls turned to look at him. Anna's breath caught in her throat. "He's got a gun," she said in a shaking voice.

"Yeah, that's right," Steve growled. "And this gun says that we don't need to involve the sheriff in this little adventure."

"Steve!" Pete cried out. "Think about what you're doing. You'll never get away with this!"

"Sure I will," Steve replied in the same cold voice. "A few guys back in town aren't quite as *upstanding* as the three of you. They'll help me get the dimes out of here."

Steve waved the gun at them. "But right now," he went on, "I've got to put you folks out of commission for a while. Take this rope, Pete. Tie the girls up. Then I'll tie you up."

Pete thought fast. "Okay, Steve, take it easy," he said soothingly. "I'll tie them up, just like you said."

Pete tied up Toni first, then Anna.

"All right, Pete," Steve said roughly. "It's your turn. Get on your knees with your hands behind your back," he snapped. Then he tightly bound Pete's hands and feet.

"There," he said. "That ought to hold you until I get back."

"And then what?" Pete asked. "Are you going to leave us out here to die?"

"That depends on just how bad you want to live," Steve snarled. "Maybe you can gnaw your way loose. Either way, I'll be long gone and far away, living in luxury!"

A few minutes later they heard the roar of the pickup's engine.

■ ■ ■

"What are we going to do?" Toni whimpered.

"Don't worry," Pete assured her. "We're going to be okay."

Then he twisted his body around toward Anna. "Pull on your ropes, Anna," he said softly. "Steve wasn't paying attention when I tied you up. When you pull on them, the knots should come loose pretty easily."

Working at the ropes, Anna asked, "Where

did Steve get that gun?"

"From me," Pete said apologetically. "Or at least from my truck. Some of the wildlife around here can be dangerous."

"Yeah," Anna grumbled. "And some of the *humanlife*, too." Finally freeing herself, she untied Toni and Pete.

"I'm really sorry about this, girls," Pete said. "I haven't known Steve for very long—I had no idea he was such a rat! But he's going to have a nasty surprise waiting for him when he gets back to town." With that, he pulled his cell phone out of his pocket.

"Darn it!" Pete groaned. "No signal. Let's just get as far away from here as we can to avoid Steve and his buddies."

"Wait a minute," Anna said. "Give me your phone, Pete."

A few moments later, Anna was once again climbing up the canyon wall to the eagle's nest. Soon she was sitting crosslegged in the middle of the aerie.

Anna popped open Pete's cell phone and looked at the display. "*Yes!*" she cried out.

Then she quickly dialed 911. "Hello? I'd like to report a robbery and attempted murder," she said to the dispatch operator.

■ ■ ■

Home at last, Anna and Toni walked through the door of the convalescent hospital. It was their first day back on the job. They stopped suddenly when they heard the sound of cheering voices: "*Surprise! All hail the conquering heroes!*"

The surprised girls were ushered into the sun room. There they were greeted with more applause by staff members and patients. Pinned on the wall was a display of newspaper articles. Several included pictures of Toni, Anna, and Pete shaking hands with the Silver Springs sheriff.

A tiny, gray-haired woman shuffled over to the girls. "We were afraid you might not come back," she said, "now that you're rich and famous."

"We *did* get a reward," Toni said, "but,

believe me, we're far from rich."

"That's for sure," Anna added. "And I think we've already used up our 15 minutes of fame."

There was a merry twinkle in the old woman's eyes. "What about that handsome young cowboy in the picture with you?" she asked.

Anna blushed. "Well," she said, "he *did* say that he'd sure like to visit California someday."

"Yeah," Toni added. "And he also promised to bring along a few of his cowpoke friends for me, too."

The two girls looked at each other, laughed, and jumped into a high five. Life was good!

After-Reading Wrap-Up

1. Because of her love of wildlife, Anna knows a lot more about animals than Toni does. On what subject are you especially knowledgeable? Name something you know about that subject that most people don't know.

2. Anna guessed that the robbers might have led the posse on a "wild goose chase." What do you think that means?

3. Anna says that bald eagles were only recently taken off the "threatened species" list in the United States. What might happen to an animal species that wasn't adequately protected?

4. Steve tells Pete and the girls that he has to put them "out of commission" for a while. What does it mean to be "out of commission"?

5. Why did Steve order Pete to tie up the girls? Why didn't he do it himself?

6. Which character in the story did you like best? Which did you like least? Explain your reasons.